For Oliver Thomas ~ P.H.

For Imogen, the new kid on the block ~ J.L.

tiger tales
5 River Road, Suite 128, Wilton, CT 06897
Published in the United States 2020
Originally published in Great Britain 2020
by Little Tiger Press Ltd.
Text by Patricia Hegarty
Text copyright © 2020 Little Tiger Press Ltd.
Illustrations copyright © 2020 Jonny Lambert
ISBN-13: 978-1-68010-210-9
ISBN-10: 1-68010-210-9
Printed in China
LTP/1400/1334/0420
10 9 8 7 6 5 4 3 2 1

For more insight and activities,
visit us at www.tigertalesbooks.com

NOW YOU SEE ME

NOW YOU DON'T

by
Patricia Hegarty

Illustrated by
Jonny Lambert

tiger tales

I am **Chameleon**.
I do as I please.
I can play tricks,
and nobody sees.

Take Elephant there—
she thinks I'm a rock . . . .

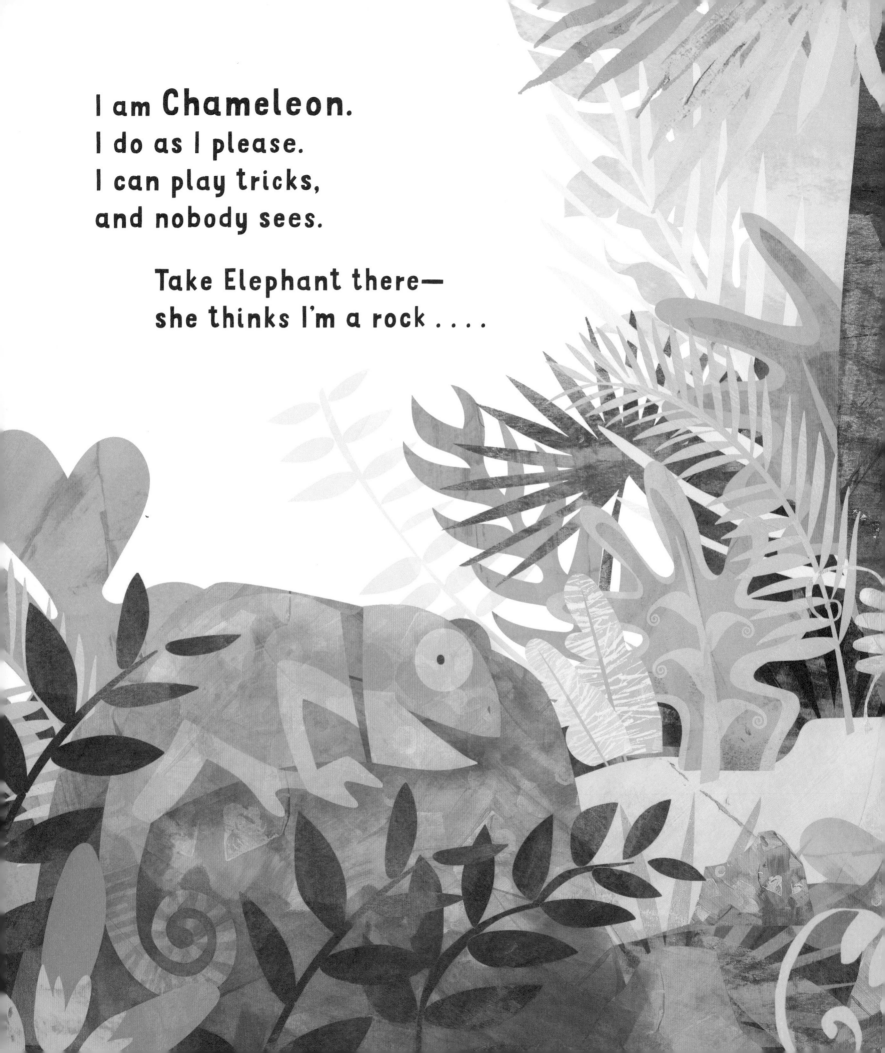

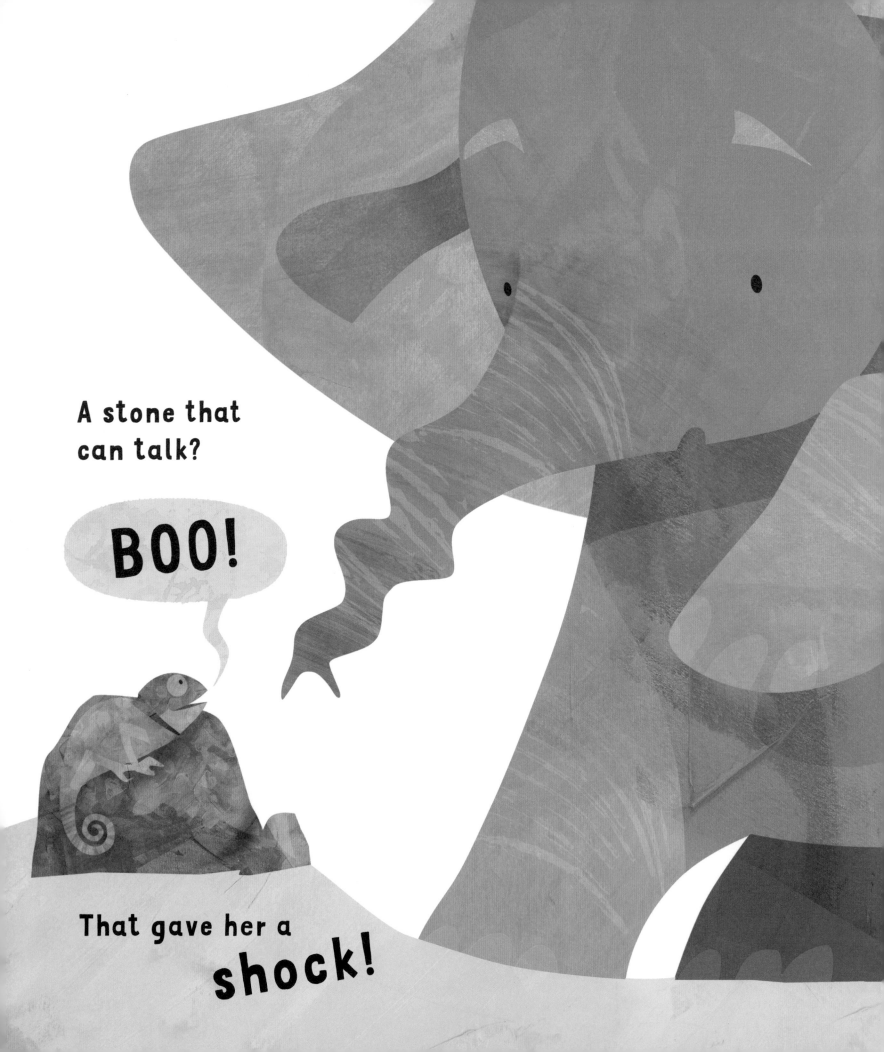

How do I do it?
It's **easy** as pie.

I can **change** color
in the blink of an eye.

When there's work to be done,
I just disappear.

Chores are for **bores**,
but not me—I'm not here!

It's bedtime for all
except cool dudes like me.
It's hard to tuck in
someone you **can't see!**

If I'm craving a snack,
I just take my pick.
I **LOVE** a banana—
look at this trick!

There's fun to be had
with this **feathery** pair....

SQUAWK!

PLUCK!

I didn't do it!
I wasn't there!

I'm feeling **INVINCIBLE**!
Now what should I do?
A sloth, fast asleep?
It's too good to be true!

TICKLE
TICKLE

Whee! Down he goes,
with a bump and a lurch . . .
And bounces Anteater
right off of his perch.

Tee-hee! Poor fellow!
Look at him go!

He's going to land ...

. . . on Jaguar!

UH-OH.

There's a horrified gasp
as all turn to see . . . .
But Frog disappeared—
all eyes are on ME!

So Frog got me back,
and now I can see:
It isn't so funny
when the joke is on me.

My camouflage tricks
are a thing of the past,
And everything's peaceful
in the jungle at last.